S0-BCM-528

LIONEL MESSI VS. PELÉ

BY JONATHAN AVISE

SportsZone

An Imprint of Abdo Publishing
abdopublishing.com

abdopublishing.com

Printed in the United States of America, North Mankato, Minnesota
102017
012018

THIS BOOK CONTAINS
RECYCLED MATERIALS

Cover Photos: Manu Fernandez/AP Images, left; Gene Kappock/NY Daily News Archive/Getty Images, right
Interior Photos: Manu Fernandez/AP Images, 4–5; Focus on Sport/Getty Images, 5; AP Images, 6–7, 15, 17; Francesco Pecoraro/AP Images, 9; Gregorio Borgia/AP Images, 11; Clint Hughes/AP Images, 12–13; Thanassis Stavrakis/AP Images, 14; ullstein bild/Getty Images, 18–19; picture-alliance/dpa/AP Images, 20; Nick Potts/Press Association/URN:31781910/AP Images, 23; Ray Howard/AP Images, 24–25; Hassan Ammar/AP Images, 26; AlterPhotos/Sipa/AP Images, 28

Editor: Patrick Donnelly
Series Designer: Sarah Winkler

Publisher's Cataloging-in-Publication Data
Names: Avise, Jonathan, author.
Title: Lionel Messi vs. Pelé / by Jonathan Avise.
Other titles: Lionel Messi versus Pelé
Description: Minneapolis, Minnesota : Abdo Publishing, 2018. | Series: Versus | Includes online resources and index.
Identifiers: LCCN 2017946926 | ISBN 9781532113567 (lib.bdg.) | ISBN 9781532152443 (ebook)
Subjects: LCSH: Soccer players--Juvenile literature. | Soccer--Records--Juvenile literature. | Sports--History--Juvenile literature.
Classification: DDC 796.334--dc23
LC record available at https://lccn.loc.gov/2017946926

TABLE OF CONTENTS

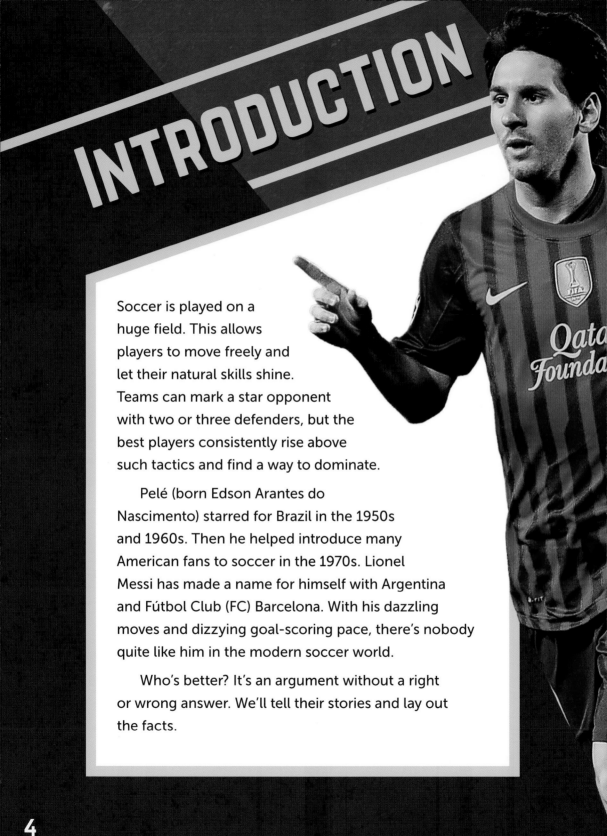

INTRODUCTION

Soccer is played on a huge field. This allows players to move freely and let their natural skills shine. Teams can mark a star opponent with two or three defenders, but the best players consistently rise above such tactics and find a way to dominate.

Pelé (born Edson Arantes do Nascimento) starred for Brazil in the 1950s and 1960s. Then he helped introduce many American fans to soccer in the 1970s. Lionel Messi has made a name for himself with Argentina and Fútbol Club (FC) Barcelona. With his dazzling moves and dizzying goal-scoring pace, there's nobody quite like him in the modern soccer world.

Who's better? It's an argument without a right or wrong answer. We'll tell their stories and lay out the facts.

MESSI OR PELÉ? YOU DECIDE!

Pelé excelled at finding creative ways to score goals.

CHAPTER 1

SCORING

Pelé began scoring goals as a professional soccer player at an early age. And he never looked back. He made his debut for Brazilian club Santos FC at 16. It didn't take long for the teenage soccer sensation to score his first goal. More than 1,200 more would follow.

The goals came during his 17-year career with Santos. He also starred in Brazil's bright yellow jerseys on the world's biggest soccer stage, the World Cup. And late in his career, Pelé became one of the first international soccer stars to venture to the United States.

Pelé is one of the greatest goal scorers that world soccer has ever seen. In fact, he might have scored more goals than any player in history, though it's hard to be sure. Record-keeping wasn't very consistent early in his career. But if there was a way to put the ball in the net, Pelé found it.

He used an accurate, powerful shot to beat goalkeepers. He could beat defenders with his tricks and dribbling. And despite standing only 5 feet, 8 inches tall, Pelé was adept at heading the ball. He could leap high into the air and seemed to hang above defenders. Then with a powerful snap of his neck, he'd head the ball into the net.

Pelé once scored eight goals in a game for Santos in 1964. But his most famous moments came when playing for his country. He was a just a teenager at his first World Cup in 1958. But that didn't stop him from collecting the second-most goals in the tournament. The scoring barrage included a hat trick in his second World Cup game. He followed that with two more goals in the final as Brazil won its first World Cup.

Argentina's Lionel Messi isn't a big man, either. Hulking defenders tower over the star of FC Barcelona and Argentina. Standing just 5 feet, 7 inches tall, how could this little guy find his way through to the goal? Any way he pleases, it seems.

Take, for example, what might be Messi's finest goal. It came in 2007 in the semifinal of the Spanish league cup. Messi, just 19 years old, picked up the ball at the halfway line. The little left-footer hopped through tackles from three defenders as he charged down the field. Sixty yards (55 m) later, after beating two more defenders, Messi faked the keeper. Alone in front of the net, he banged it home for the goal.

Jaws dropped. Fans and teammates cheered. It was, his fellow Barcelona forward Deco said, "the best goal I have ever seen in my life."

In the years since teenage Messi's wonder goal, there has been no shortage of others. By age 25 he was already Barcelona's all-time leading scorer. He achieved that milestone in 2012, the same year he broke a scoring record that seemed untouchable. Messi scored 91 goals combined for Barcelona

Messi had to get used to playing against opponents who were much bigger and stronger than he was.

MEET THE PLAYERS

PELÉ

- Born October 23, 1940, in Três Corações, Brazil
- 5 feet, 8 inches/150 pounds
- Youth club: Bauru Athletic Club (1954–56)
- Home today: Guarujá, São Paulo, Brazil

LIONEL MESSI

- Born June 27, 1987, in Rosario, Argentina
- 5 feet, 7 inches/159 pounds
- Youth clubs: Newell's Old Boys (1994–2000) and FC Barcelona (2001–04)
- Home today: Barcelona, Spain

and Argentina's national team that year. The previous record for goals in one calendar year was 85, set by Gerd Müller of Bayern Munich and West Germany in 1972.

Messi made his first-team professional debut in a friendly in 2003. Since then he has scored more than 600 goals for club and country. Only his rival Cristiano Ronaldo—star of Real Madrid and Portugal—has approached his scoring pace in that time.

What makes Messi such a splendid scorer? He is deceptively quick, able to burst past defenders with ease. His ball control is elite. It allows him to keep the ball close and fire off shots where others cannot. And Messi is among the best finishers in the world. He can put a delicate touch on shots that slip past goalkeepers just as easily as he can curve a blasted shot over a defensive wall on a free kick.

The only way Messi doesn't score often is with his head. But even so, he has netted a famous header. Barcelona led Manchester United 1–0 in the 2009 Champions League final when Messi found space near the net. A pass sailed in from the right and Messi rose to meet it. He headed the ball into the back of the net and clinched Barcelona's third European cup title.

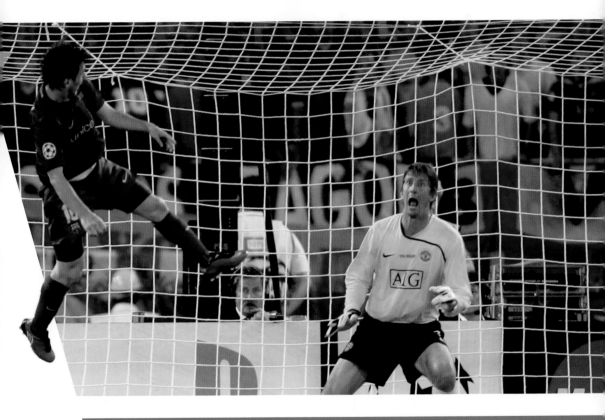

Messi stuns Manchester United with a header for a goal in the 2009 Champions League final.

Agility and concentration pay off as Messi beats Manchester City's Yaya Toure in a 2014 Champions League match.

CHAPTER 2

FIELD SKILLS

Barcelona trailed visiting Real Madrid 1–0 in April 2017. A win would all but clinch the league title for Madrid. Messi wouldn't hear of it.

Messi collected a pass just outside the 18-yard box. His lip was already bloodied by a collision with an opponent's elbow. Now surrounded by defenders, he controlled the ball and took one touch to accelerate toward the goal.

A forest of legs stood between Messi and the goal. Messi tapped the ball and darted left, past the wall of white-shirted Real Madrid defenders. The goalkeeper rushed toward him. But with one final touch of the ball, Messi sent it firmly into the back of the net.

Three touches within 15 yards displayed the skills that make Messi among the best soccer players in the game. His delicate touch, quick acceleration, and ability to see everything around him set him apart.

Messi leaves two Panathinaikos defenders in his wake in a 2010 Champions League game.

And Barcelona went on to win, on a last-minute goal by Messi, no less.

As big as it is, a soccer field can get crowded. Twenty outfield players fight for possession and space. Messi's genius lies in his ability to see and find space where others cannot. And when he attacks that space, he maintains possession of the ball better than any other player.

FC Barcelona recognized his talents right away. After a tryout with the club in 2000, it signed Messi away from his boyhood club, Newell's Old Boys, in Argentina. The boy nicknamed "The Flea" for his small size and style of play signed his name on the back of a napkin.

"In two minutes, I saw his speed, his skill, and decided we would sign him," Barcelona's technical director told a reporter. "He will become the best in the world."

Creativity and skill made Pelé nearly impossible for opposing defenders to handle.

PROFESSIONAL SUCCESS

PELÉ

- First professional match: September 7, 1956
- Years active: 1956–77
- Team trophies won: 26
- World Cup appearances: 4 (1958, 1962, 1966, 1970)

LIONEL MESSI

- First professional match: November 16, 2003
- Years active: 2003–present
- Team trophies won: 29
- World Cup appearances: 3 (2006, 2010, 2014)

That's a title that Pelé has long held. The Brazilian star was unstoppable in so many ways. He had the raw skills to overpower defenders. He could also leave them confused by his deft touch with the ball. Pelé could embarrass defenders at will. And frequently he did.

Pelé is most famous for all the goals he scored. But his ability to create chances for teammates shouldn't be overlooked. With back-heels and accurate passes into space, he could make defenders scramble.

The abilities to find space and beat defenders with his dribble helped Pelé bag an enormous number of goals. Those skills helped him create space and scoring chances for his teammates, too.

At the 1970 World Cup, Pelé put all these skills on display. Finally healthy after being injured in each of the previous two

World Cups, he played brilliantly in Mexico that summer. His dribbling through and around opponents left defenders lying on the ground in his wake. After getting Brazil on the board with the first goal in the final against Italy, he delivered a perfect ball to Carlos Alberto, who scored Brazil's fourth and final goal. It was an exclamation mark on the country's third world title and Pelé's final match for Brazil.

"He was such a talented player with great control and vision," said England legend Bobby Charlton. "He read the game and he read positions. He had an arrogance but not in a bad way. He was a great player, so why shouldn't he strut a little bit?"

Pelé holds off a defender in a fight for possession.

Pelé, *center*, celebrates with the Jules Rimet Trophy in 1970 after leading Brazil to its third World Cup title.

CHAPTER 3

TROPHIES

Rising from a boyhood in Bauru, Brazil, to his throne as *O Rei* ("The King") was a long climb for Pelé. He was born into punishing poverty in 1940. He began to play soccer not with a ball but with rolled-up socks. By the time he was 15, though, he had signed with the Brazilian club Santos. And it didn't take long for Pelé to start collecting trophies.

He won his first major title with Santos in 1957–58 when the club captured the championship of the top league in the state of São Paulo. With Pelé leading the team, Santos would win that competition nine more times over the next 12 years. Five titles in the Brazil Cup tournament followed, too.

Pelé had grown into a superstar. He had led Santos to the most successful period in its history. And international glory followed for both his club and country.

Pele, just 17 years old, pressures the France goal in the 1958 World Cup semifinals.

Santos won its first South American continental competition in 1962. The Copa Libertadores draws the best soccer clubs from across South America. Pelé led a talented team to its first Libertadores final, where it played Uruguayan power Peñarol.

With his club clinging to a 1–0 lead, Pelé made sure his team would leave as winners. He exchanged passes with a teammate at the edge of the penalty area as he looked for space to shoot. Then he pounced. A rocket by Pelé into the net made it 2–0. He added another goal in the game's final seconds, and Santos was the champion of South America.

Pelé was just a teenager when he first took the field for Brazil at the World Cup in 1958. That's when the young prodigy exploded onto the world soccer scene. He netted six goals in the tournament, including a second-half hat trick in the semifinal against France and two more while defeating host Sweden to clinch the trophy.

All the success came with a price. Opponents went after Pelé with brutal play in the 1962 and 1966 tournaments. Brazil won the 1962 World Cup, but Pelé was on the bench with an injury. He was injured again in 1966. This time Brazil bowed out early. That experience left Pelé thinking he was done with the World Cup. But he decided to come back for one more in 1970. Many say Pelé and Brazil were never better. He scored four goals on the way to a third Brazilian title.

Messi, on the other hand, didn't seem destined for similar greatness. He grew up small and fragile. He was diagnosed with a growth disorder. On his first day of class as a kid in Rosario, Argentina, the other boys left him out of a schoolyard soccer game. He took the field anyway and showed off his skills. He had no trouble getting chosen to play after that.

When he was 13, Messi moved to Barcelona. The club paid for the expensive medical treatments he needed to grow. His first-team debut came three years later, in 2004.

Since then, nearly all Messi and FC Barcelona have done is collect trophies. The club won eight Spanish league titles

PELÉ

- World Cup goals: 12 (in 14 matches)
- Career highlight: At the age of 17, Pelé scored six goals as Brazil won its first World Cup.
- Awards won: World Cup Best Young Player, 1958; World Cup Golden Ball, 1970; Ballon d'Or Player of the Century
- World Cup record: 12 wins, 1 draw, 1 loss, 3 championships

LIONEL MESSI

- World Cup goals: 5 (in 15 matches)
- Career highlight: In 2014–15, Messi scored 58 goals as Barcelona won the Spanish league and cup and the Champions League title.
- Awards won: Ballon d'Or, 2009–12, 2015; Di Stefano Trophy (best player in La Liga), 2009–13, 2015; World Cup Golden Ball, 2014
- World Cup record: 11 wins, 2 draws, 2 losses, 0 championships

between 2004 and 2017, the most successful period in club history.

But team success is just part of the story. Messi also has collected personal honors at a furious pace. The Ballon d'Or is awarded each year to the player voted the best in the world. He has won the trophy a record five times, including four in a row from 2009 to 2012. The award was established in 1956, but only European players were eligible during Pelé's playing days.

But despite all his club success, there's one important hole in Messi's résumé. With Argentina he is winless in four international finals as a senior player. In 2014 Argentina reached the World Cup final, only to fall to Germany in extra time. They lost the Copa América final on penalty kicks in 2015 and 2016.

Messi was heartbroken after the defeat in 2016. Shocking fans, he announced his retirement from international soccer. "It's been four finals, and I was not able to win," he said. "I tried everything possible. It hurts me more than anyone."

But a few months later, Messi was back in the blue and white, trying to win an elusive title for Argentina.

Messi holds the Champions League trophy after leading Barcelona to the title in 2011.

Pelé goofs around with New York Jets star quarterback Joe Namath in 1975.

CHAPTER 4

STARDOM

Reporters, television cameras, and fans packed into a room in a New York City restaurant on June 10, 1975. The world's most famous athlete had just signed a contract with one of the local teams and was about to be introduced to the media.

But the star athlete wasn't a golden-boy quarterback, an ace pitcher, or a high-flying basketball player. It was Pelé. *O Rei.* The King.

In the United States in the early 1970s, professional soccer was dying. The top US pro league, the North American Soccer League (NASL), had few stars. Teams struggled to draw fans, and the league received little attention from the media. All that changed when the New York Cosmos signed Pelé in 1975.

Pelé had already been a huge international star for many years. His Brazilian club, Santos, barnstormed

When Brazil hosted the 2014 World Cup, even stars like David Beckham, *right,* lined up to have their picture taken with Pelé.

across the globe, playing in front of millions of fans. Many major European clubs such as Manchester United and Juventus tried to lure him away. But the Brazilian government passed a law that declared Pelé a national treasure. That meant he couldn't leave Brazil to play professional soccer. Still, Pelé managed to make his mark on the world stage just the same.

PELÉ

- Important records: Considered the world's all-time leading scorer with 1,280 goals in 1,363 games
- Key rival: Diego Maradona (Argentina) was considered Pelé's only competition for the title of greatest player ever.
- Off-field accomplishments: Has been a Global ambassador since his retirement; was appointed to a United Nations commission on the environment; has worked to reduce corruption in Brazilian soccer

"I sometimes feel as though football was invented for this magical player."

—England star Bobby Charlton

LIONEL MESSI

- Important records: Most goals in a calendar year with 91 in 2012
- Key rival: Cristiano Ronaldo (Portugal and Real Madrid) has dueled with Messi for nearly a decade to be the best player in the world.
- Off-field accomplishments: Works with UNICEF to help vulnerable kids around the world; started the Leo Messi Foundation to increase access to health care, sports, and education for kids

"Messi is an alien that dedicates himself to playing with humans."

—Juventus goalkeeper Gianluigi Buffon

Finally, in 1975, Pelé was 34 and near the end of his career. The Brazilian government gave him its blessing to sign with the Cosmos. And American fans flocked to the stadiums to see the global superstar. Television networks broadcast the league's games and brought Pelé's style and skills beaming into American living rooms, too.

"The biggest challenge for us," Cosmos teammate Werner Roth once told a reporter, "was not stopping and watching him play."

Messi has benefitted from playing in the mass media era. Cable and satellite TV are filled with 24-hour networks devoted to

Messi's No. 10 Barcelona jersey is the most popular in the world.

sports, including many that focus on just one sport. Fans in the United States can watch live games from Europe, Asia, and South America. Then they flock to social media to share clips of the latest amazing goal or save. The sport has never been more popular worldwide, and much of that growth can be traced to amazing players such as Messi. His famous No. 10 Barcelona jersey is sold more than any other in the world. The little magician has become one of the world's biggest stars.

Much of Pelé's glorious career took place in black and white. Many fans only read about his feats in the pages of a newspaper. Messi has bloomed in full color. The highlights of his heroics are just a YouTube search or weekly Champions League broadcast away.

You can call up his highlights and watch him dribble past six opponents. Then watch him dance through defenses and arc the ball in a high flick over a flat-footed goalkeeper. Or check out his Instagram posts, where he shares moments from his life with his 77 million followers.

His appearances in the 2016 Copa América Centenario tournament in the United States played like one long highlight reel. Crowds forked over more than $100 to see Messi's Argentina team play rival countries from throughout North and South America. He didn't disappoint, coming off the bench to score three goals against Panama. The fans in Chicago knew they were witnessing greatness. Even when he wasn't on the field, their chants filled the air: "MESSI! MESSI! MESSI!" Like Pelé before him, Messi excelled at thrilling American soccer fans.

GLOSSARY

CLUB
The team a player competes with outside his or her national team.

DEBUT
First appearance.

FREE KICK
A way of restarting play after a foul. A player may shoot or pass with the opposing defense a set distance away.

FRIENDLY
A match that is not part of league play or a tournament; an exhibition match.

HAT TRICK
Three goals by the same player in one game.

HEADER
A technique used in soccer to control, pass, or shoot the ball using the head.

PENALTY AREA
The box in front of the goal where a player is granted a penalty kick if he or she is fouled.

PENALTY KICK
A free kick at the goal, defended only by the keeper, awarded after a foul in the penalty area; also used is shootouts to break ties in some competitions.

RIVAL
An opponent with whom a player or team has a fierce and ongoing competition.

TACKLE
A defensive move to take the ball away from another player.

ONLINE RESOURCES

Booklinks
NONFICTION NETWORK
FREE! ONLINE NONFICTION RESOURCES

To learn more about great soccer players, visit abdobooklinks.com. These links are routinely monitored and updated to provide the most current information available.

MORE INFORMATION

BOOKS

Logothetis, Paul. *Lionel Messi*. Minneapolis, MN: Abdo Publishing, 2016.

McDougall, Chrös. *The Best Soccer Players of All Time*. Minneapolis, MN: Abdo Publishing, 2015.

Trusdell, Brian. *Pelé: Soccer Star and Ambassador*. Minneapolis, MN: Abdo Publishing, 2014.

INDEX

ABOUT THE AUTHOR

Jonathan Avise is a reporter, writer, and digital media editor from Minneapolis, Minnesota. An avid soccer fan, he is a die-hard supporter of North London's Tottenham Hotspur.